Who is AC?

Hope Larson

illustrated by Tintin Pantoja

Atheneum Books for Young Readers
NEW YORK LONDON TORONTO SYDNEY NEW DELHI

ATHENEUM BOOKS FOR YOUNG READERS
An imprint of Simon & Schuster Children's Publishing Division
1230 Avenue of the Americas, New York, New York 10020
This book is a work of fiction. Any references to historical events, real people, or real places are used fictitiously. Other names, characters, places, and events are products of the author's imagination, and any resemblance to actual events or places or persons, living or dead, is entirely coincidental.

Also available in an Atheneum Books for Young Readers paperback edition
The text for this book is set in CCBlahBlahBlah.
The illustrations for this book are rendered digitally.
Manufactured in China
First Edition
10 9 8 7 6 5 4 3 2 1
Library of Congress Cataloging-in-Publication Data
Larson, Hope.
Who is AC? / Hope Larson ; illustrated by Tintin Pantoja. — 1st ed.
p. cm.
Summary: "Meet Lin, an average teenage girl who is zapped with magical powers through her cell phone. But just as superpowers can travel through the ether, so can evil. And as Lin starts to get a handle on her powers (while still observing her curfew!) she realizes she has to go head to head with a nefarious villain who spreads his influence through binary code"—Provided by publisher.
ISBN 978-1-4424-6540-4 (hc)
ISBN 978-1-4424-2650-4 (pbk)
1. Graphic novels. [1. Graphic novels. 2. Superheroes—Fiction.] I. Pantoja, Tintin, ill. II. Title.
PZ7.7.L37Who 2013
741.5'973—dc23 2011052616

Who is AC?

June 15, 2013
"Lower your sword," cried the bandit king.

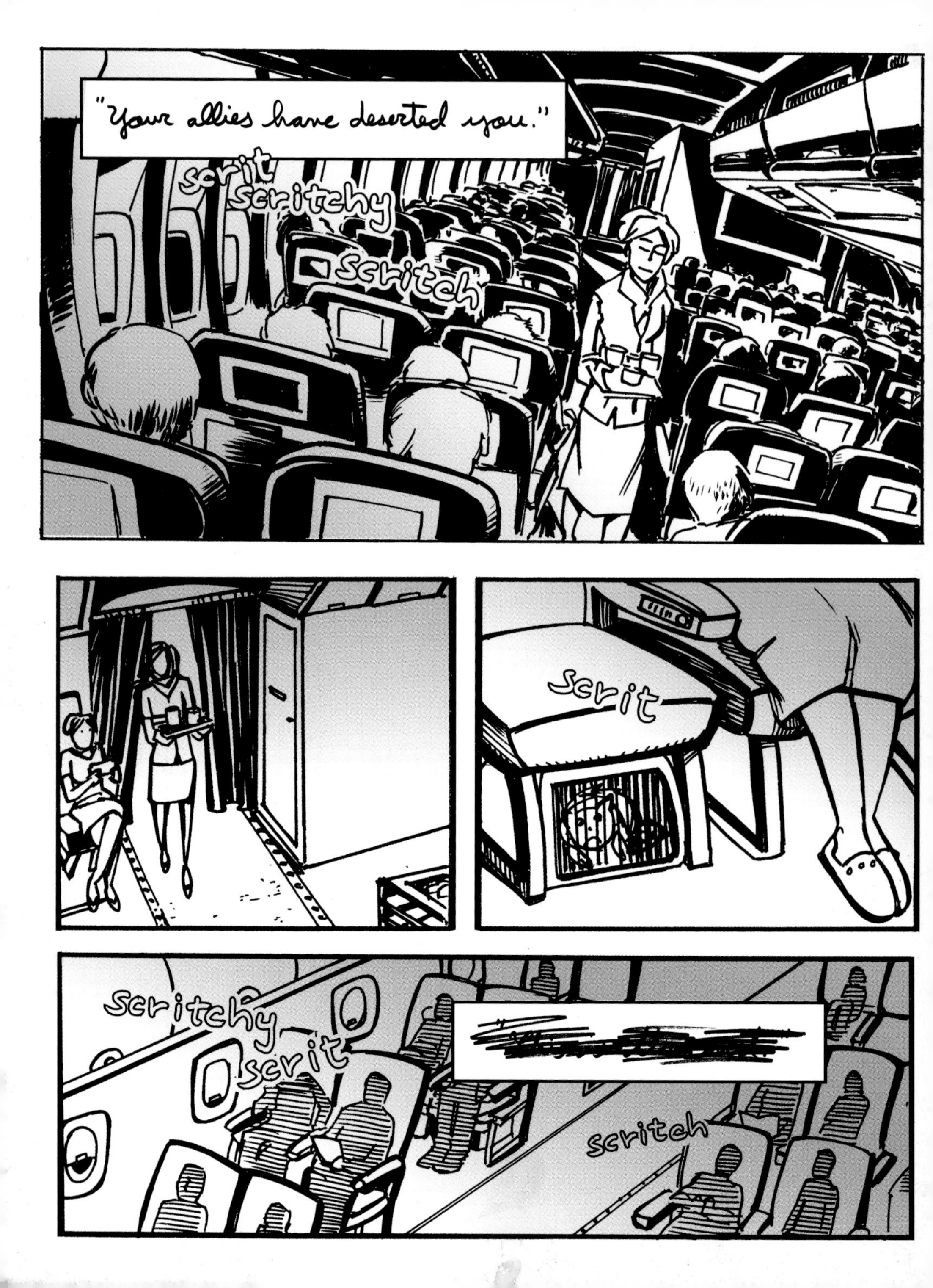
"Your allies have deserted you."
scrit
scritchy
scritch
scrit
scritchy
scrit
scritch

Hm . . .
scritch
Rhea rolled her eyes. "So?"
scritchy
scrit
green velvet, the
last vestige of her
days at court. She
could no longer
hear her comp-
anions' footsteps.
arrow grazed
shoulder & she
around,
Ancilla at the
ready, her bright
steel flashing.
"Lower your sword,"
cried the bandit
king. "Your allies
have deserted you."
Rhea rolled
eyes. "So?"

"So . . ."
HALLOWEEN 2009
HALLOWEEN
HALLOWEEN 2009
So . . .

LOVE
IN THE
TIME
OF
OPE RA
Z
Z
Z

Z
Z
Z Z
Z
Z
How can they sleep? So unfair.

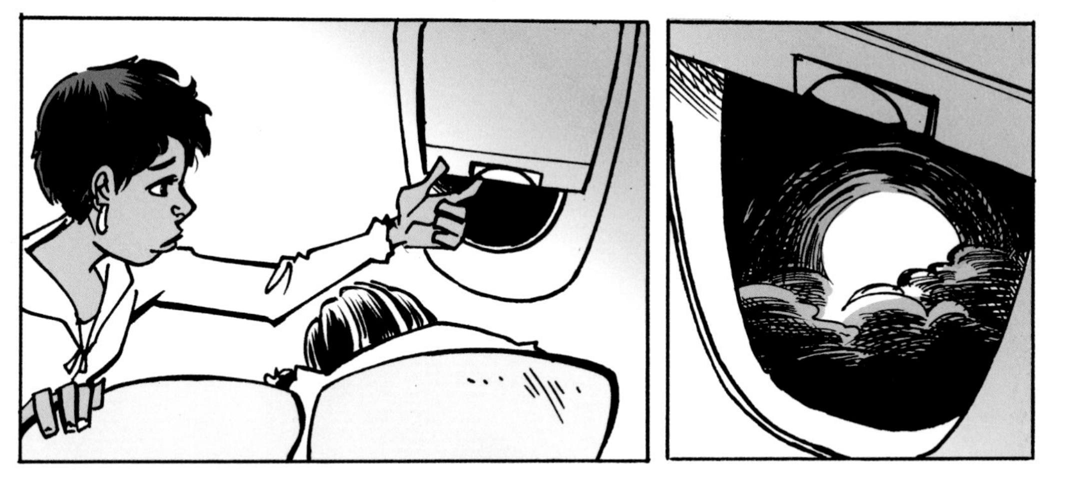

I miss you guys already.

Yeep!
BZZ BZZ!
No way-
BZZ BZZ!
My phone can't possibly be ringing at thirty-five thousand feet!
BZZ BZZ!
Please don't let the plane crash because of me!
BZZ BZZ!

KACHUNK!
OCCUPIED
BZZ BZZ!
Incoming Call from 00101111 01101111 01101101 01100101
Huh?
BZZ BZZ!

BZZ
BZZ!
Uh . . .
Uh,
hello?

. . . and we wish you a pleasant stay in New York, or wherever your travels may take you. *CLICK*
Lin? Wake up, Lin! We're here!
Wha . . . ?
Nnnooooo!
Granola bar? You slept through breakfast.
Uhhh . . . No thanks. Not right now.

Jerry?
Harv?
Granola bar?
YAAAAWN
No, thank you.
Can we have sushi later?
Mm . . . I don't know, Harvey.
I remember going to the bathroom, but . . .
There might not be a sushi restaurant in Barnhurst.
Because it's so far from the ocean?
?
No, Harv- because it's so far from civilization.
Sigh.
Jerry . . .

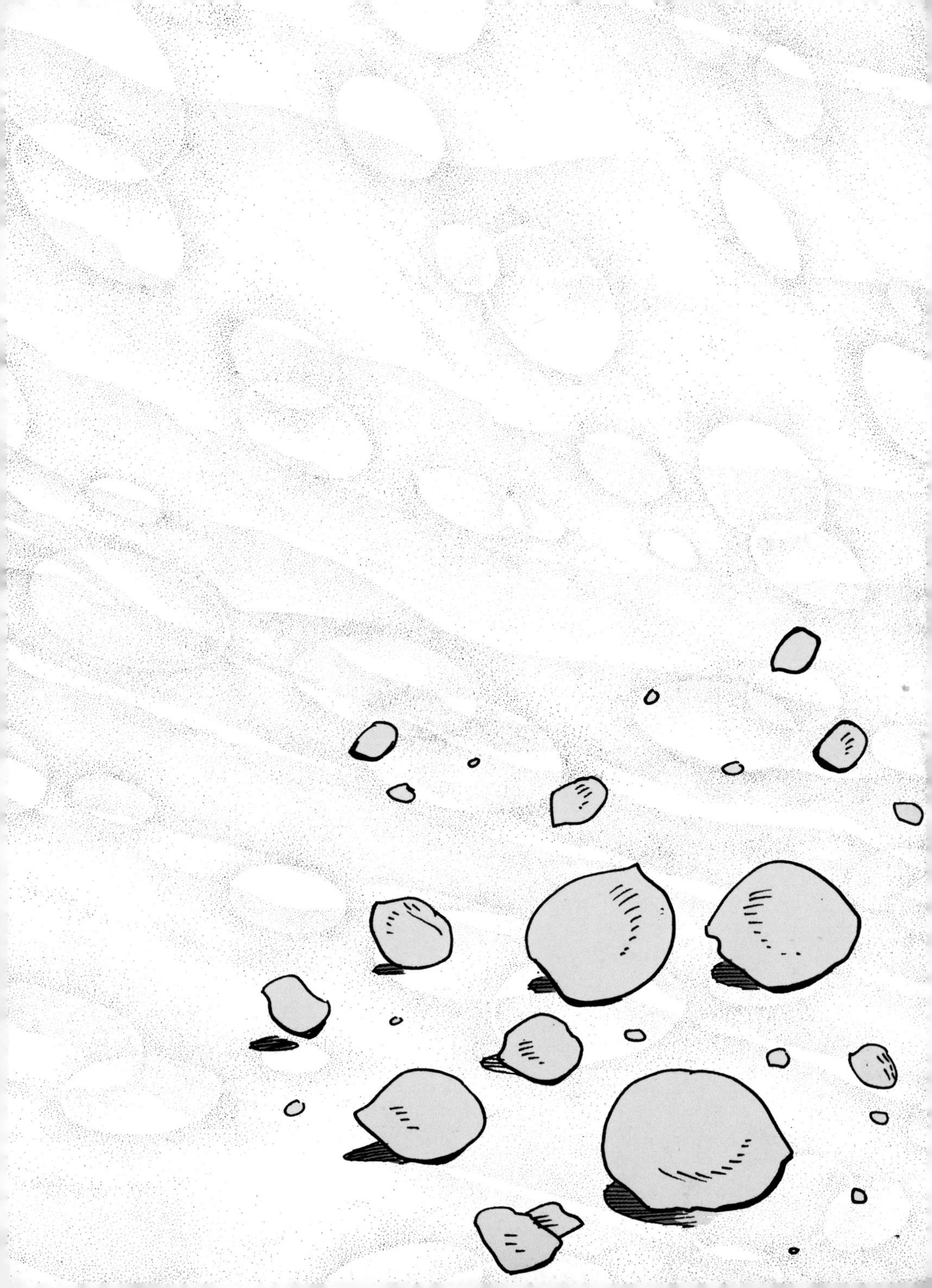

I'm going, Dad!
Okay!
Who is AC

August 23, 2013
chirp
skree
skree
Friday
Welcome to
BARNHURST
Pop. 2,647
HISTORIC DOWNTOWN ↑
SHOPPING ↑
BARNHURST COLLEGE ↑

WELCOME FIGHTING PORCUPINE
WELCOME FIGHTING PORCUPINE
CANDY CLOUDS
SALE
BARNHURST PLAZA
BARNHURST PLAZA
SHOPS · DINING · PROMENADE

5X FAST
PHOTOCOPIES · INTERNET
PHOTOCOPIES
So, six thirty?

Seven.
It's my last day, so of course Dora's keeping me late.
5x FAST
PHOTOCOPIES · INTERNET
I got a customer. See you at seven!
5x FAST
PHOTOCOPIES · INTERNET
OLD TYME
PHOTOGRA
Okay!

She's lecturing till ten? On a *Friday*? Brutal.
So . . . can I eat out?
BANNERS
Okay, it's a deal. Skim?
Two percent.
No, Dad, I got it covered.
See you at nine! Byyye!

?
GLUE
Need a hand?
COPIES
BINDING
Nope. Got it covered.
Oookay, well . . .
Lemme know if that changes. I'm off soon, but for now I'll be right over there.
My name's-

OLD TYME
PHOTOGRAPHY
Trace?!
Trace Vernon, Mel?
Really?
Really.
Pff! He's a jerk.

He's in my class, and he seriously has no friends.
Mm.
Once, he actually-
I don't want to know. Okay, Dora?
He's always been nice to me.
Whatever. I just thought, since you go to St. Emillionaire's-
St. Emily's.
-you should know what you're getting into.

Thanks for the intel. Zip me?
I like your perfume.
Huh?
No, it's . . . I probably smell like hay.
Hay?

Later . . .
An' how 'bout you, sweetie?
BARNHURST DINER
DINER
DINER TURKEY SPECIAL 10.99
The, uh . . . the house salad and a Diet Coke, please.
I'll be right back with your drinks.
It must be hard, being a girl.
What? Life?

Growing up brainwashed by the media, thinking you've gotta be thin, look a certain way . . .
DESSERT
It's a salad, Trace, not a cry for help.
Oh, uh . . . I didn't . . . I wasn't talking about you.
KA-

KA-CHUNK!
"I WAS THERE AND JUST RETURNED:" THE TRAVELS OF RHEA IRONHEART.
You done?
Yeah, finally.
Too bad. It's cool watching you work. You've got, like, a whole system.
BHL

So that comes to . . . uh . . .
$30.87.
Here's thirty, and I think I've got the eighty-seven.
Have a good night!
Take it easy.
GLAM SALON
5X FAST

Ride safe, girlie.
Leavemealone!

BARNHURST PLAZA
He wasn't waiting for me.
...

THRIFTY MART
Um-
BURRITO
SPICY JALAPEÑO
If I buy this, you'll nuke it for me, right?
Yeah.
MILK
Cool. Then I'll take it.

beep
beep beep
beep
MILK
BURRITO
TOTAL
$5.18.
Okay~
EMPTY

Stupid,
stupid,
stupid,
BARNHURST PLAZA
SHOPS·DINING·PROMENADE
stupid!
At least that sketchy van's gone.
Oh *no*.

5X FAST
PHOTOCOPY · INTERNET
OLD TYME

Relax.
This isn't even, like, a crime- it's just desperation.
O-Okay.
I mean, I got thirty grand of debt for a degree I can't use. Now my extortionist dentist says I need, like, a root canal, and what am I supposed to do?
Are . . . Are you asking me?
Heh. No, man.
You're a kid. What do you know?

What do I *do*? Call the cops?
They'll never make it in time!
Oh God, I'm *useless!*
Anyone else would've saved the day by now.
You like your job, kid?
Worked here long?

Only my whole life. My uncle owns the Plaza, so basically I'm an indentured servant.
But at least I'm not putting tourists in petticoats.
I can't believe I thought that'd be fun. What's wrong with me?

No Sig
What's wrong with me?! I've got to do something, right?
What am I supposed to do?

00101111
01101101
01100101

00101111
01101101
01100101
00101111
01101101
01100101
Calling . . .

TAK
TAKKA
TAKKATA
TAK
TAK
TAKKA
TAK
You!
NET HUT
NET HUT

TAK
TAKKA
TAK
TAKKA
TAK
You're up and running at last!
I admit, I'm relieved. I'd begun to think you wouldn't come, and you know how I worry.
TAKKA
TAK
TAK
Was it a pleasant trip? Uneventful, I hope. I'm dying to hear about it, but first, tell me-
/whois
00101111
01101101
01100101
Where did you land?
TAK
TAK
TAKKA
TAK
TAKKA
TAK
TAKKA
TAK
TAK
TAKKATA

Barnhurst?!
Well, hello, neighbor.
FAST
Thanks for your help, uh . . .
Uh, Pete.
5

And hey, if you noticed any ways I could, like, improve the whole robbery experience . . .
I'm totally open to feedback.
TING!
S-Sailor Moon?!
Um . . .
0:03

No! I'm-
uh-
Who?
Nevermind
who I am!

GASP

NO!
THWOK!
No, no-
OOF!

Stay.
Got any packing tape?

So this wasn't so bad.
You mean tonight?

Yeah.
Well . . .
Could've been worse.
I mean, I didn't think you'd come. You seem to be in pretty high demand.
BA-DUM!
Pff. I wish!

No, but what about that Hunter guy?
Are you still seeing him?
Who told you about Hunter?
Who? Oh, uh, the Internet.
You read my blog?
Gotta scope out my competition.
Well, don't worry.
Oh, I wouldn't say I was *worrying* so much as-

Shut up, Trace.
CLINK

He's dead.

Thought you might need a box.
Yeah, well, I don't.
SPLORK

BARNHURST DINER
BARNHURST
Diner
sniff

WHEW!
Thanks!
Am I supposed to, like, tip you?
I don't think so. . . .
POSTE
Do you need any copies?
gift certificate
?
Nah. I should get going.

5
PEN
You better keep an eye on him till the cops get here.
I . . . I will.
Later, Pete.
FAST

2:50
Two minutes, fifty seconds. Not bad!
END

huh
huh
huh
Get a grip, Lin!

What a rush!
That happened, right?
There's no way that happened.

I better try it again.
Just to be sure.
01101101
01100101
Calling . . .
Meanwhile . . .
Jeez, those're some headlights. . . .

Huh?!
What the-Flower petals?!
?
Aaaaa!
Aaaaaaaaaaa!

THUMP!
DOGGY BAG
SQUISH
@#%*!
Huh?

CLICK

WRRRRR

You're home early. How was the date?
Fine.
Did you make her cry?
Will we be getting an angry call from her parents?
I don't know! Probably!
HA HA HA HA HA HA HA
And by the way, I lost my glasses. Thanks for noticing.

F16
GO! FIGHTING PORCUPINES
Girls, man.
I bet Mel's blogging about me right now. Can't wait to read all about what a-
What a jerk I am.
Boys.

I hate boys. Hate 'em.
Hate my life. Hate this blog.
tAK
tAK
tAKKAtA
D from work? Hate. She thinks I'm so spoiled, but it's not like I fit with the rich kids! And she freaks out when I date, like that's worth getting jealous about.
I mean, boys-and PS I hate boys-just see me as a trophy. Most of them.
Hunter got it. He got me.
Now he's gone.
tAK

I should probably delete this, but I've written the same things before. And before that. Over and over.
I wish I could take it all back, from the beginning.
I wish I could just disappear.
Bip
Huh?
CHIT•CHAT
Melly, you have an invitation to chat.
/me
ACCEPT
DECLINE

/me
ACCEPT
Click
/me
ACCEPT
Melly
Uh . . .
Hello?
/me
Hi. I saw
your blog.
You seem
upset.
Melly
Trace?
No.
Who is this?
Unimportant.
/me
Oookay . . .
Listen, Melly
I can make y
disappear.

That's impossible.
It isn't.
Not for me.
Heh.
From the Internet, at least. Erase those overshares, those moments of weakness.
I can erase your digital shadow.

CANTERBURY BOOKS AND NEWS
Howdy, Lin. Lookin' rough. Late night?
YOUR SOUR FOR BACK T SCHOOL
SALE
You know me . . . just making the most of summer.
School starts Monday.
Yeah? Hey, wanna hear something wild?
Uh . . .
ROSES
Are bodily fluids involved?

Lin.
Lin! You're my favorite customer! You're here every week!
I'd never say anything that might damage this . . . this beautiful thing between us.
What, my money?
You buy a *lot* of hardcovers.
Anyway, my news is, I totally have Art History Survey with your mom.
That's it? I'm disappointed.
You kids, so blasé. Like *your* life's a thrill a minute.
Actually . . .
I WAS THERE AND BACK AGAIN—THE ADVENTURES OF RHEA IRONHEART
VOLUME TWO
BY
LIN CARRO
Ta-daaa!
I can leave these on consignment, right?
Ooo, part two!
We haven't sold out of part one, but hey, sure.

You only sold-
One.
Some girl bought it.
CLOUDS
ZINES & COMICS
Here's your cut.
FLIP
...
PAT PAT
Don't feel bad, kiddo.
I'm fifteen!

And you're *good* for fifteen!
You read it?
Sure!
You owe me another 50 cents.
Heh heh. Want some advice, Lin?
Nope!
OPEN
Too bad! Here goes: Print is dead. Go start a blog!

A *blog*? Like I'm that desperate.
BARNHURST CHRONICLE
TODAY WE GO DIGITAL!
BARNHURST
GULP!

Whaaa?
We got held up?!
GO! FIGHTING PORCUPINES!
The Barnhurst Sentinel
our exclusive video!
NEW GIRL IN TOWN
Mystery heroine prevents holdup, vanishes
BED HEAD
Employee Pete Levin described the masked do-gooder as "cute, but intense."
Man. Where was she when I lost my glasses?
After disarming and restraining Jason Campbell, 25, a former student at Barnhurst College, the woman left.
She was just gone!

Perhaps strangest of all is the large amount of white rose petals that littered the crime scene. Levin had no explanation, but was happy to speculate.
Could be she's a florist.
Florist . . . ?
It's her! The girl from . . .
from . . .
PHOTOS
downloading . . .
You crashed my bike!
You!

I don't know who you think you are . . .
. . . but *you're going down!*

BARNHURST PUBLIC LIBRARY
Okay. So.
Rhea Ironheart, marooned on a desert isle by her traitorous fiancé . . .

Noooooo!
Hmm?
No!
Shh!

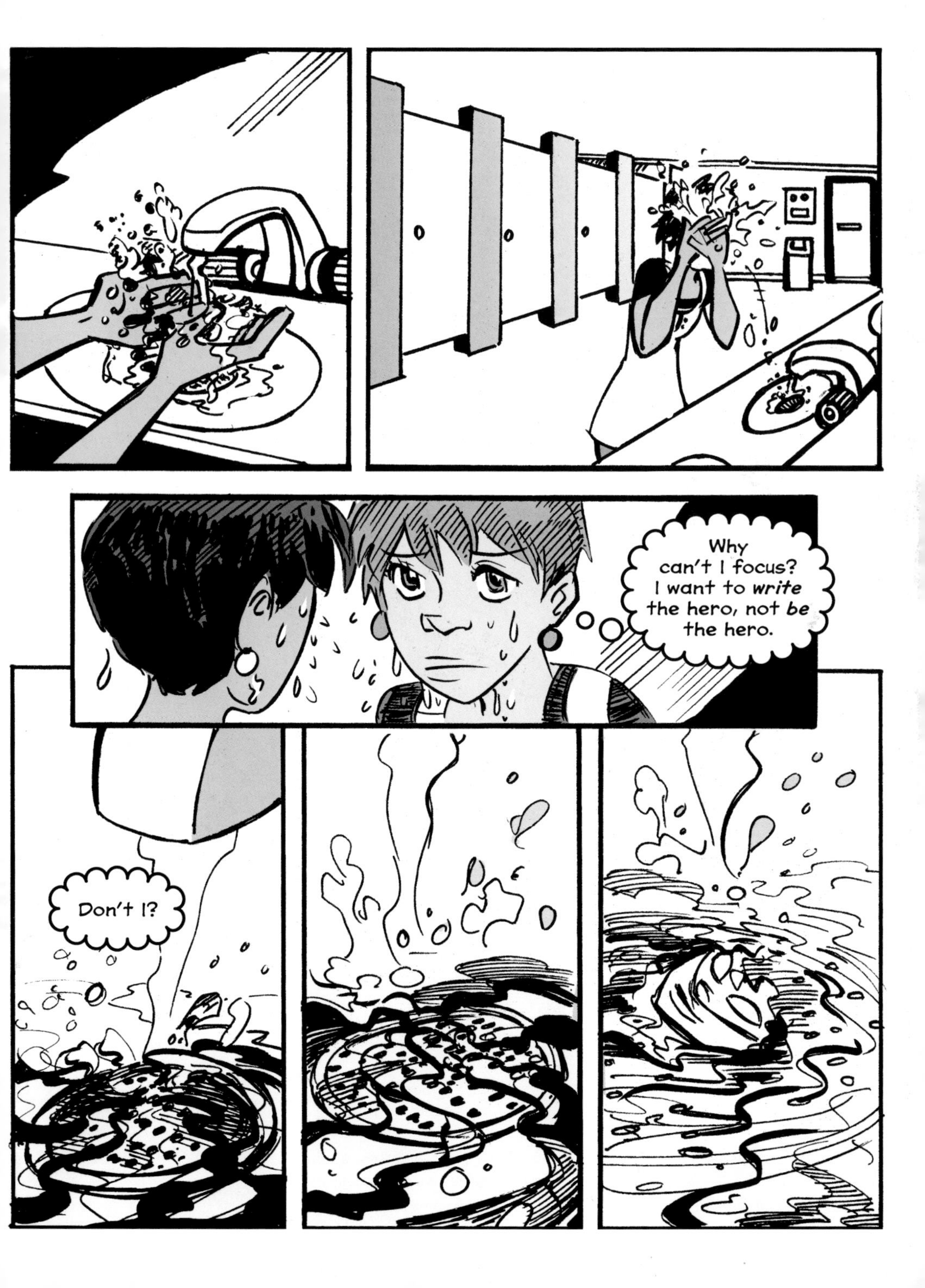
Why can't I focus? I want to *write* the hero, not *be* the hero.
Don't I?

TAK
TAKKA
TAK
TAKKA
TAKKA
TAK
Inspired.
@}-^-v---
MYSTERY HERO
or
ANONYMOUS COWARD?
@}-^-v---
On the night of the holdup at
Fast Copy
and not
publicit
a stunt
so-calle
bicycle
Roa
On the night of the holdup at 5x Fast Copy Shop . . .
. . . if it was a holdup and not a stunt staged for publicity, the so-called "Mystery Hero" caused a bicycle accident on the old Field Road.
Although no one was seriously hurt, the cyclist suffered minor injuries and damages to personal property amounting to several hundred dollars.
Our "hero" subsequently fled the scene, and has made no attempt to reimburse the victim for his loss, instead preferring to cower, anonymous, behind her mask.
Since she didn't provide a name—that is, an *alias*—let's pick one for this anonymous coward.

Anonymous Coward.
AC.
Catchy, right?
So, AC, if you're reading this . . . stay sharp. We'll be watching.
PS You owe me a pair of glasses.

WILLOW BRANCH ESTATES
EST. 2008

No one's home. . . .
Dad must be out with Harv.
Hey!
Hey, you!
Me?
Yes, you! Come over!
You live in the last house?

Yeah?
Cool! That was my great-uncle Frank's house.
He died there and everything.
C-Cool . . .
Yeah. He was the only one who wouldn't sell when the developers came through.
Ooh. Hard core.
POP
That's his bike, too.
Oh! Do you need it back? It was in the shed, so I just . . . And I mean, the brakes are out, so . . .
Nah. It's no big deal.

SSSLURP...
So I'm Kay.
I'm Lin.
CHER OP
Lin . . . Carroll?
Yeah?
OhmyGod! Wait right there!

Hey.
I'm Mel.
Melly.
I like to ski and watch horror movies. And I ride. Do you ride?
Horses? Nope . . .
And I'm Team Edward. What team are you?
Hahaha . . . Uh . . . No team. I'm kind of a free agent.

That's so cool.
We should be friends.
Um.
I know we just met, but I feel like I know you.
Can I tell you a secret?
!
Uhhh . . .
Th-This is kind of a bad time.
Actually, I-

Huh?!
Use the light! Let the light protect you!
Here goes . . .

Listen, Melly-
I can make you
disappear.
Relax, Lin.
Lighten up.

We're all friends here.
Hahaha ha!

Call me! Text me!
Don't be a stranger!
I have to go!
What. Was. That?!
Lin!

Aw.
She left?
Yes,
Kay....
Oh.
Well, anyway, you've got to read this! Lin wrote it, and it's, like, completely amazing.
I WAS THERE AND BACK AGAIN- THE ADVENTURES OF RHEA IRONHEART
VOLUME TWO BY LIN CARROL
Reading's not, like, one of my interests.
I WAS THERE AN BACK AGAIN-THE ADVENTURES OF RHEA IRONHEART
VOLUME TWO
I'm going home.

A whole day, and you haven't found me one new follower?
I'm disappointed, Melly.
I tried, but Kay doesnt have a shadow at all! Not enough of one to hold on to. And what'shername, Lin . . . I almost had her, but she got away.
No excuses! You didn't try hard enough. You're nowhere near as likeable as I thought you'd be.
Ouch.
That boy-Trace. Call him.
But I hate him!
Yes, and he hates *her*. With that hate, that anger, he has the potential to become a troll of great power.
So *you* talk to him.
He wouldn't trust me. You, though . . .

Call him. That's an order. With him on your side, uncovering AC's true identity and stripping her of her power will be child's play.
Ha!
Who said that?!
No one's out there . . .
Rrgh! I know!
We're done here.
Well? Get out of here! Go!

I'm sorry, Trace, but we've discussed it, and that's our answer.
But I need glasses for school!
If you'd been more responsible with the first pair-
Boy, if you'd taken better care of your eyeballs, you wouldn't need glasses at all.
What?! It's not my fault I have lousy vision!
If you spent less time reading and playing computer, we might not be in this situation.
Just sit at the front of the class, Trace.
Right. With the kiss-ups.
Here's hoping their work ethic rubs off on you. . . .

Fine.
If you need your glasses, you'll just have to go out and find them.
Why don't you check the garage, Trace? I remember packing an old pair with your eighth-grade things.
Oh! Quick, dear, the game's on!
CRUNCH

So how was your day? Sell any chapbooks at the book shop?
Chapbooks? Are you serious? They're called *zines.*
FOOM!
I sold one whole copy.
?
That's a great start, Lin!
Don't patronize me, Dad. I'm not stupid.
Oh no! Life as the dinosaurs know it has been destroyed!

Well, maybe it's the title, hm? It's a bit, uh, long, don't you think?
This from the author of *Symbols of Gender Discontinuity in the Sculpture of Central American Social Realists of the 1930s.*
That's my *thesis*, Lin-It's totally different.
The academic community is cool with that sort of thing.
Right. And how *is* the ol' thesis going these days?
At this rate you'll have your master's before I do.

Thanks for helping with the dishes. You're excused.
...
Okay.
Play with us, Linny!
We're playing ELE.*
Not now, Harvey.
*Extinction-Level Event
The Travels of Rhea Ironheart. That could work.
Or just *Ironheart*. Dramatic!
Or . . .
STOMP!
Sigh.

BEEEP!
BEEEEEP
What now?
C'mon, I *just* charged you!

About time you plugged in your phone.

I've been trying to connect for an *hour*, Lin. An *hour*.
How could you let your battery get so depleted?
Don't you know what's at stake?
It takes an awful lot of juice to bring me over, and-
AIEEEE!
CRASH!

Lin . . .
Are you okay?
See? Nothing to fear. I couldn't hurt you if I wanted to.
I can't even help you up.

Lin?
NOK NOK
Um, I'm okay, Mom!
Well, all right . . .
She's gone.
So, what now? Who are you? Why are you in my room?
Ahem.
I am Pollux, your dispatcher.
I'm not a taxi service.
No, but you're a . . .
a . . .

Sigh.
I hate to put a label on it. . . .
By all means, "Pollux," label me.
Hero, warrior, agent of justice . . . Take your pick.
I don't like any of those.
Look, it doesn't matter. There's a troll on the loose.
A troll? How fun.
Yes.
How fun for you.
Hey!
You're on call.

TRACE'S STUFF
TRACE'S STUFF
Man. I was so . . . *accomplished*. What happened?
Oh. Right.

Aha!
I said, "*Phone*," Trace!
Huh? No one calls me on the house line!
Just take it, Trace! I'm missing the game!

Hello?
Trace? Hi. It's Mel.
Couldn't stay away, huh?
Guess not.
Can you come out?
Out?
I need to talk to you.
Uh . . .
I promise it's nothing bad.
O . . . kay. Well, where should we meet?
Thorny Hill.

click
Horny Hill?
You, sir, are irresistible to women.
Guess it runs in the family.

TV GUIDE
I'm going out to find my glasses.
Fine.
Umhmm.
Just don't be clompin' up the stairs in the middle of the night. Mom and I have church in the morning.
Yeah. I know.

THORNY HILL
PARK

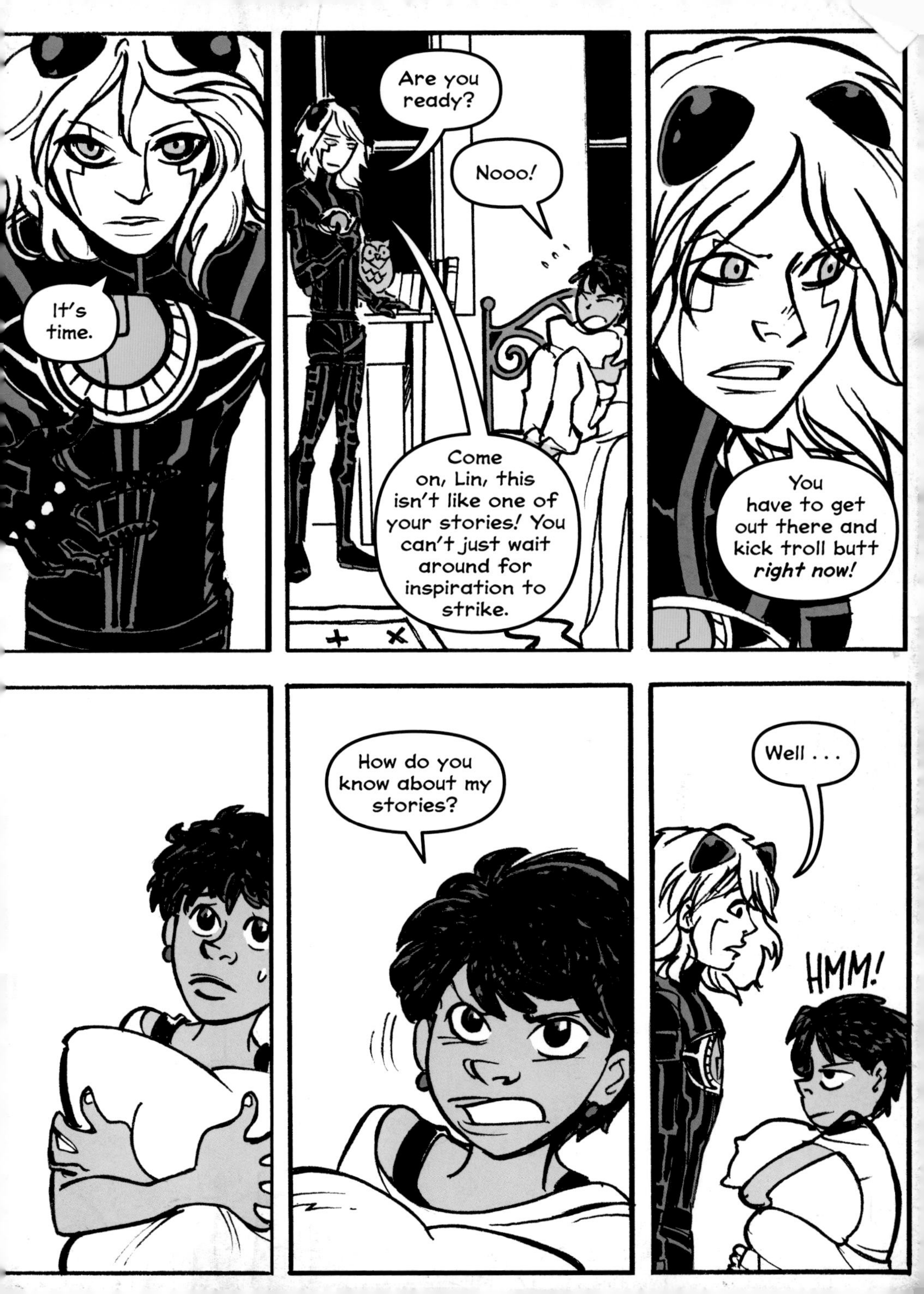
It's time.
Are you ready?
Nooo!
Come on, Lin, this isn't like one of your stories! You can't just wait around for inspiration to strike.
You have to get out there and kick troll butt *right now!*
How do you know about my stories?
Well . . .
HMM!

No. That's for later. We haven't got time.
If you don't deal with this now, you'll really be in trouble. You're nowhere near ready to deal with him.
"Him" who?
Our enemy, /me.
You?
Not *me*, Lin. */me*. Now, please, stop stalling, suit up, and get out of here!
I dispatch thee! Shoo!
Where are you dispatching me *to*?

Thorny Hill.
Okay, but I seriously doubt I'm ready to-
Relax. You'll know what to do.
It's all in your program.
My *what*?

I'm heading out for some air.
At this hour?
Uh, yeah! I'm . . . I'm stuck on a scene.
smek!
Well, wear a coat. It's getting chilly.
Yes, ma'am!

Show 'er who's boss, Lin!
W-What?
The muse.
Oh. I'll try.
And be back in an hour!
Okay!
KITCHEN
She takes her writing so seriously, Pam.
?

She's a kid. She should be out doing kid stuff, but . . .
I mean, she just blew her allowance on *photocopies*.
Sweetheart, we only just got here.
Once school starts and she's made some friends, she'll tone down the poet act.
Poet act?!
Like I'd even write poetry! Poetry is for stoners!
Whatever. They'll see who's "acting" when I get a book deal at eighteen.

No, seventeen.
00101111
01101101
01100101
TAK TAK
TAK
Calling . . .
00000

THORNY HILL
PARK

Should I have brought something?
I don't even like . . .
. . . beer.

Oh, *man*. She's crying.
She's crying, and she'll want to talk about it.
This is so . . .
. . . not my problem.
CRACK!

Hiya, Mel!
I'm glad you're here. I just . . . I, *sniff*, needed someone to talk to.
And I know we just met, Trace, but I . . . I feel like I know you.
Uh . . .
So what did you want to talk about?
GERDANGERDA
GERDANGERDA
ERDANGERDAN
DANGERDAN
'Cause we've established that I suck at . . . talking.

We're friends, right?
W-What kind of friends?
I mean, you're on my list. Am I on yours?
Can I tell you a secret?
I don't get it, Mel. You flip out when I read your blog, and all of a sudden-
Shh.
It's about Hunter.
I don't wanna talk about other guys . . .
Don't worry, Trace. He's not a boy. He's a-
STOP!

Leave him alone!
Ow!
Stoppit!
It's that guy from 5x Fast! Trace. Need a hand, buddy?
What'd you do to him?!
Huh?

Nothing!
I was only *liberating* him . . .
Urk!
THWAK!
. . . from the shell of lies he's constructed for himself here in the quote unquote real world.
Wasn't how it looked to me!
If you could see who he really is . . . who he is online . . .
Ugh, enough! I'm sick of the freaking Internet!
No. No way. That's-
YOU!

BLINK
He has such potential.
And he totally hates you.

Me?
Why *me*?
Why you?
What do you think, Trace-should we tell her?
"We"?

Or *show* her?
No! Stop!
Hold *still!*
!?

Go ahead and hate me.
I'm still going to save you, 'cause I'm just-just better than you!

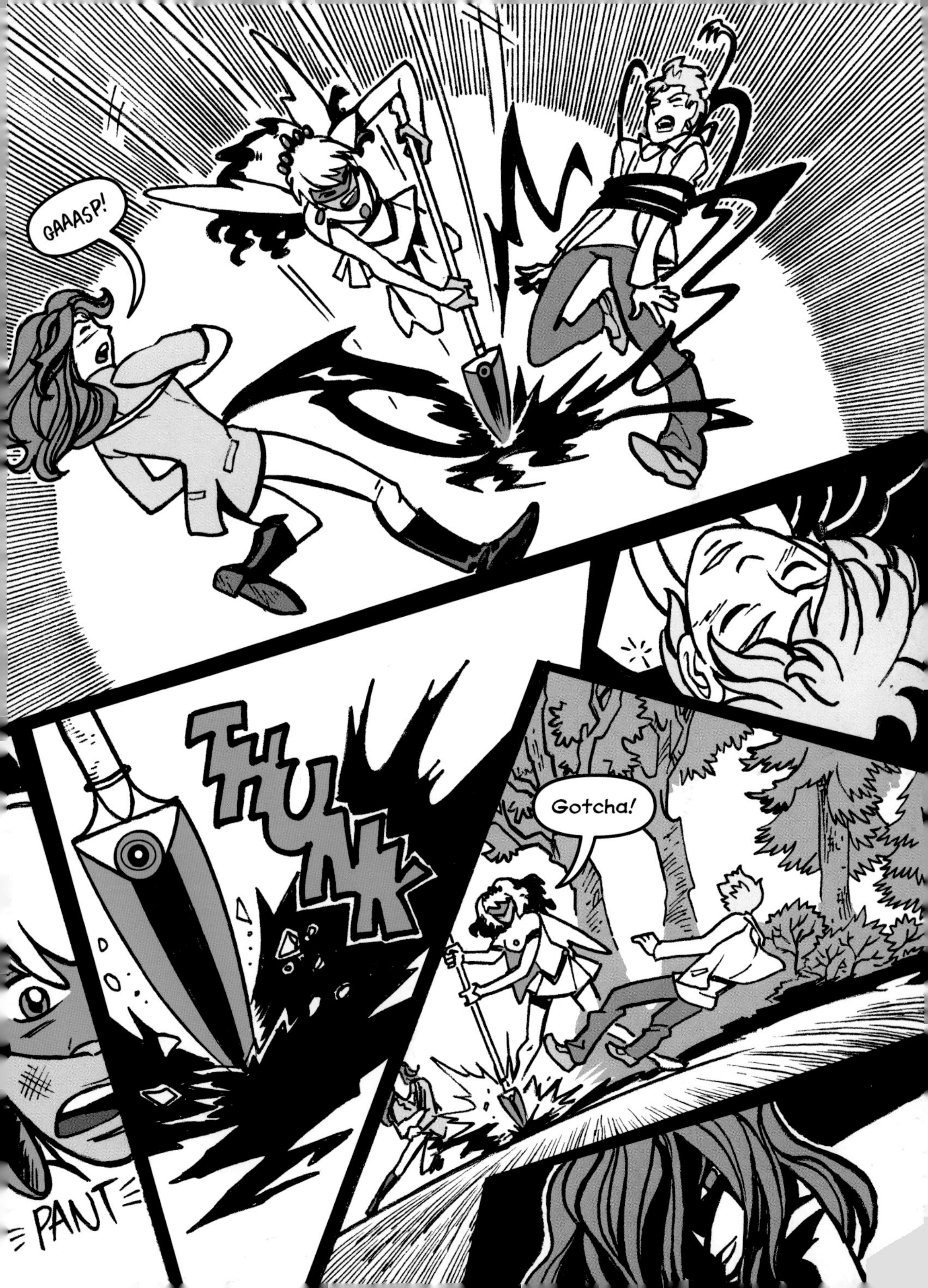
GAAASP!
THUNK
Gotcha!
PANT

You'd pick on a girl with a broken arm?
You aren't a girl at all. You aren't even real!
I'm just as real as you!
Whatever that means!
I'm still not convinced I *am* real right now or that any of this is happening.
I meant that-that I've got *feelings*!
Feelings?! You've definitely got *something*.
But *feelings* don't manifest as weird shadow-tentacles!

Feelings don't attack people!
CRINGE!
NO!
She'll get away!
!
What's wrong with you?!
You were hurting her!
You idiot! She's a troll!
"Troll" is such an ugly word.

Is that what you see in me?
My friends look at me and see money.
Boys? They just see a trophy.
Wait. I've heard this before. . . .
Hunter's the only one who understood . . .
. . . and now he's gone.
Her blog!
What?
That thing's cribbing from Mel's blog!

He's gone because of *me!*
Who's Hunter? Her ex? Fill me in.
Her, um . . . Actually . . . I think he was her . . .
Spit it out, Trace!
Her horse.
Oh.

Stop it, Mel! This isn't you!
Yes it is! This is who I really am!
It's not! This is a bunch of stuff you wrote when you were lonely or depressed or— or bored.

SSSNORT!
HISS!
Eek!
Don't worry, I'll be-
Ohhh.
Guess it's called Thorny Hill for a reason.
Don't worry, I'm not going to hurt you.

I'm just going to make you who you truly are.
You know her, right? Distract her!
Me?
Yes! I can't do this alone!
I-
I wish you'd t-tell me about Hunter, Mel!
No! That's private! I never wrote about that!

We went out riding. I knew we shouldn't go that way. I didn't think.
There was a rabbit hole, and his ankle . . . I *heard* it.
Snap.
They put him down after that. Because of me.

But that wasn't your fault!
Yeah!
Shut up!
It's gotta have a weakness, but where?
There!

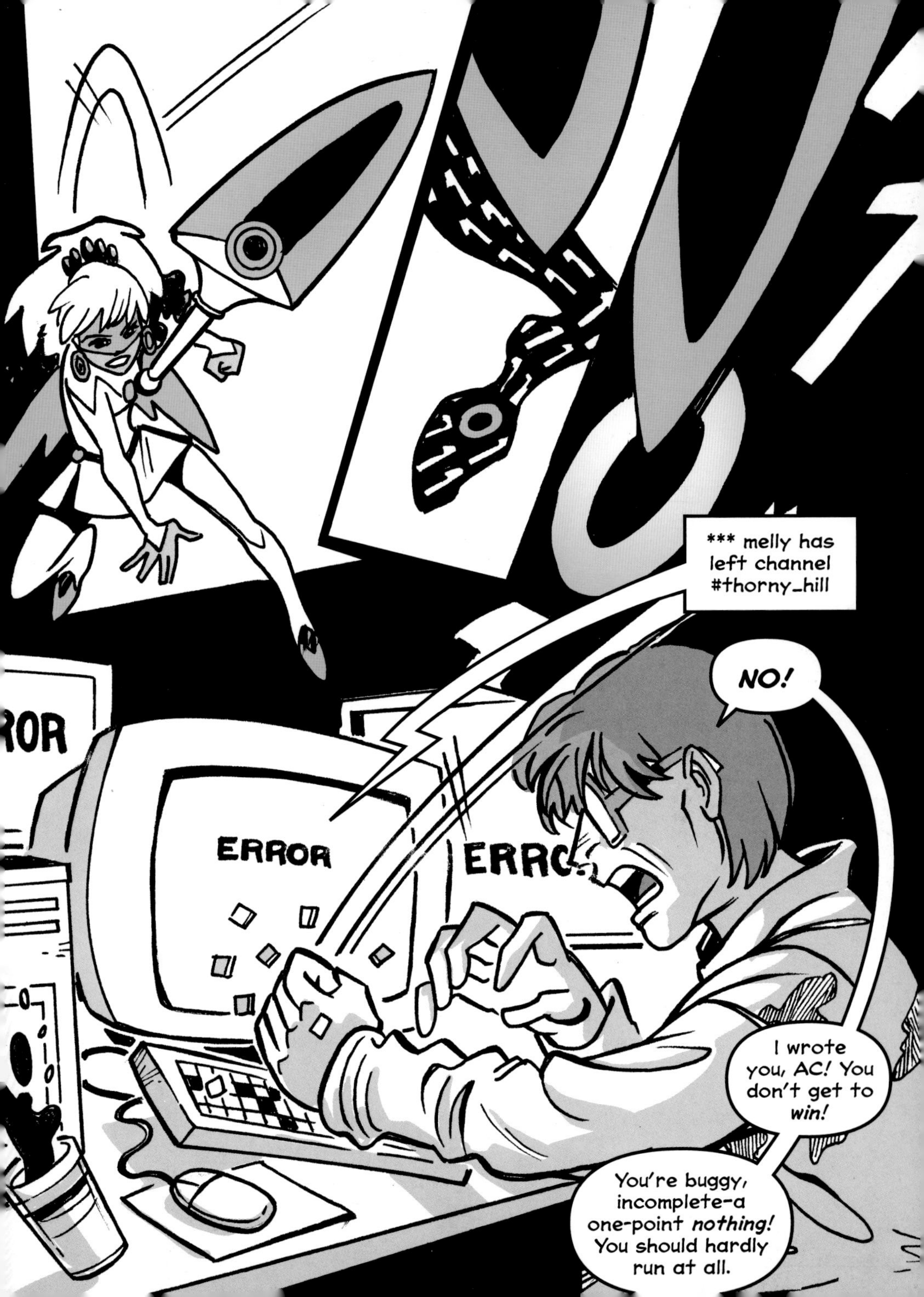

*** melly has left channel #thorny_hill
ROR
ERROR
ERRO
NO!
I wrote you, AC! You don't get to *win!*
You're buggy, incomplete—a one-point *nothing!* You should hardly run at all.

So why can't I beat you?
NET HUT
Mel!
Are you okay?
I- I think so. . . .
Where am I?
Up Horny Hill.
Trace . . . ? What are you doing here?
What happened to your glasses?
You tell me.
Shh!

Since you're friends, can you get her home?
Isn't that your job? You're the hero.
I know . . .
But I'm kind of about to blow my curfew.
Right. Whatever.
Hey, I was wondering . . .
What were you-
FLASH!

Ow.
Sorry, I wanted a candid. Okay if I post it later?
Uh . . . Where?
Worsthero dot com. Check it out.
What?
So long, AC!
?
AC?

Air conditioner?
END.

La voilà!*
And right on time. How'd it go?
Okay.
*"There she is!"
I was just about to watch The Dark Knight. Care to join me?
The Dark Knight? Um . . .
. . . maybe tomorrow.
Gonna hold you to it!
Thanks, Dad.
Any time.

I can vouch for her, Mrs.-
Ms.
Ms. Downing. No one was drinking or drugging.
Drugging? Is that even a thing?
I feel strange, Mommy. I don't think I had enough to eat today.
Think you can hold out long enough for me to make cookies?
Oatmeal?
Sure.
Care to join us, Trace?
No thanks. I'm staunchly anticookie.

Funny kid.
He's not as much of a jerk as he tries to be, I don't think.
You know, Melly, it's time you stopped punishing yourself for what happened to Hunter.
It was an accident. No one blames you.
I know. . . .
Remember Mr. Spaulding? He called today. He's selling a couple of horses, and he thinks one of them might be perfect for you.
Her name's Magnolia.
We can go by and meet her tomorrow. What do you think?
. . .

TAKKA
TAKKA
TAKKA
TAK
creeeeeeeeak

C'mon, baby, you can do it!

@}-^-v---
MYSTERY HERO
or
***ANONYMOUS COWARD*?**
@}-^-v---

On the night of the h
5x Fast Copy Shop,
a holdup and not a s
staged for publicity–
a holdup and not a s
staged for publicity,
so-called "Mystery H
caused a bicycle acc
on the old Field Roa

Although no one was
seriously hurt, the cy
suffered minor injurie
damages to persona
property amounting to several hundred dollars
"hero" subsequently fled the scene, and has n
attempt to reimburse the victim for his loss, in
preferring to cower, anonymous, behind her m

Oh, I get it. . . . Anonymous Coward. AC.
I guess that's not so bad.
Actually, I *like* it. Suck on that, Trace!
"So, AC, if you're reading this, stay sharp. We'll be watching."
Ooh, I'm scared!
"PS You owe me a pair of . . ."
glasses
Oh no.

They've gotta be here somewhere.
SIGH

F-16
2:00 AM
Hey there.
I'm glad you're still up.
What happened to your curfew?
Uh . . .

Did you come over to break some more of my stuff? Or did you just want to ask another favor?
Look, I'm sorry about earlier. This whole thing's new for me, and-
So you're an amateur.
You aren't from around here, are you? I mean, *clearly*.
What makes you think you can waltz into Barnhurst and put on some vigilante act?
It's not an act. I'm not like this on p-purpose.
Right. And by the way, 5x Fast is *my* shop. I'm the *manager*, and everything was under control before you-
What are you talking about?! You weren't even there!
I *was*.
I didn't *want* to be!
Wow, you're actually *crying*?
Please go away. I'm in the middle of a game.

Then you'll want these.
Yeah, I-
What's that? You *don't* want 'em?
Well, okay!
Argh! *NO!*

What is wrong with me?!
sniff
God, I am an amateur.
I can't believe I cried.

So, Lin, how are you spending your last day of freedom?
I don't know.
I do!
BIKE AUCTION
ARMORY TODAY!

Gasp!
BIKE AUCTION TODAY
I'm in love!

Excited for sophomore year?
I'm . . . uncertain about the uniform.
You'll be okay.
I'll be great.
Obviously.

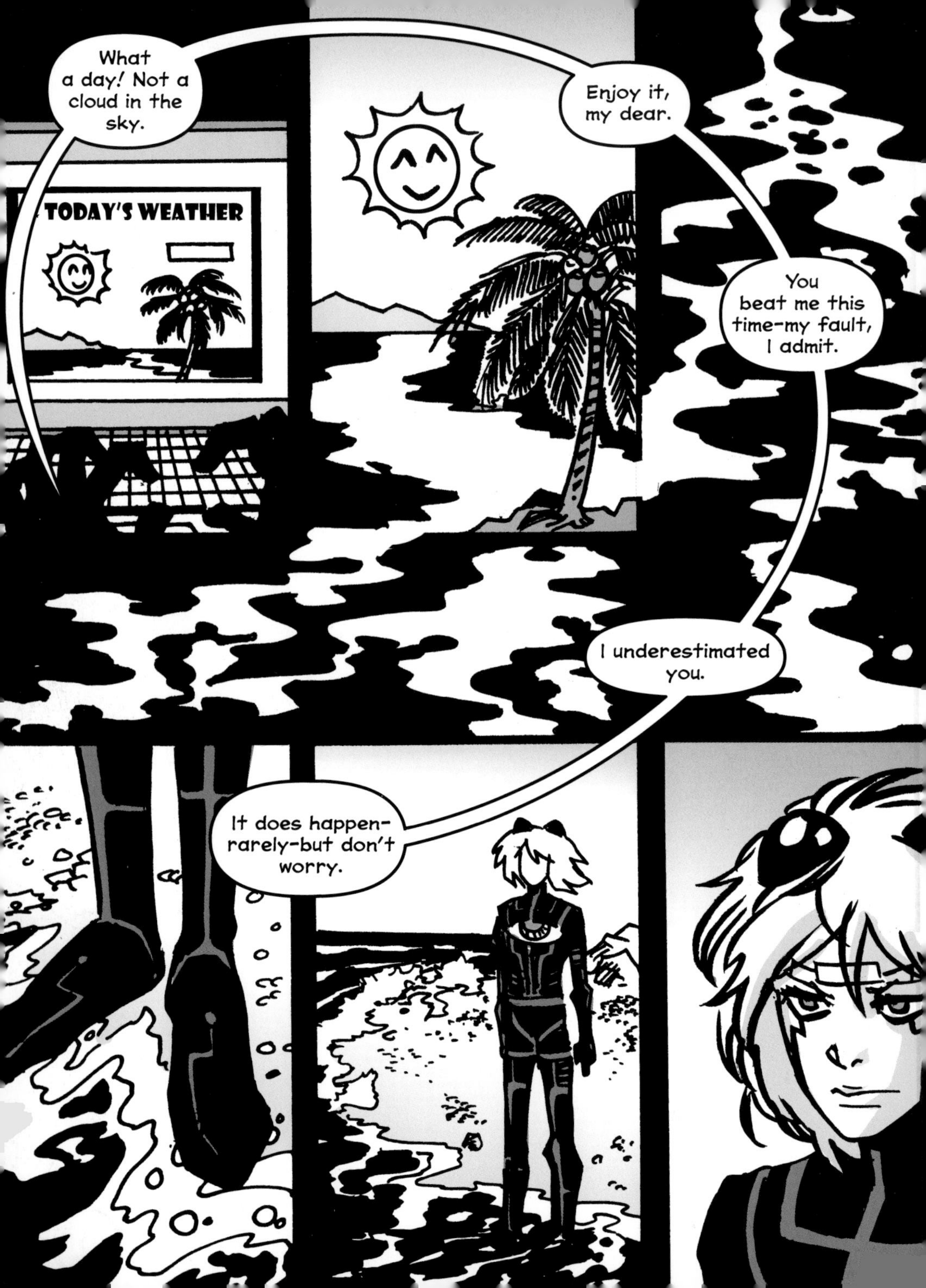
What a day! Not a cloud in the sky.
TODAY'S WEATHER
Enjoy it, my dear.
You beat me this time–my fault, I admit.
I underestimated you.
It does happen–rarely–but don't worry.

I'll be ready next time.

Hope Larson is the author of ***Mercury, Chiggers, Gray Horses,*** and ***Salamander Dream,*** which ***Publishers Weekly*** named one of 2005's best comics. She won a 2007 Eisner Award, the highest honor for a comic artist. She lives with her husband in Los Angeles. You can visit her at hopelarson.com.

Tintin Pantoja graduated from the School of Visual Arts in 2005 with a BFA in Illustration/Cartooning. Her past works include ***Shakespeare's Hamlet: The Manga Edition*** for John Wiley & Sons and three volumes of Graphic Universe's Manga Math Mysteries series. She currently resides in the Philippines. See more of her work at tintinpantoja.com.